The Lid

by Michael P. Di Gennaro
illustrated by Bruce MacDonald

 Richard C. Owen Publishers, Inc.
Katonah, New York

Whoosh!
A great gust of wind blew the lid off
Mr. Rooney's brand new trash can.

The lid rolled down the street
and past the street lamp.

It rolled under the mail carrier
and over the mail.

It rolled by the police officer
and through the red light.

It rolled in front of the market
and the shoppers.

It rolled past the firehouse,
the fire-engines, the firefighter, and the fire dog.

It rolled across the playground
past the children.

On and on and on it rolled.

It rolled all the way back to Mr. Rooney's house

and landed among the flowers.

That's how Mrs. Rooney got a birdbath
for her garden.